This book
belongs to

....

Cuddle's Fan Pages

Here's what other children have to say about their favourite kitten and her latest adventure!

"I really like Cuddle because she's magic. I liked it when she made Hypno sleepy with her tail. I like Olivia and Grace too. They're nice." Caitlin, age 7

"My favourite bit was when Chloe sang with The Krazy Katz and Cuddle played the drums. Grace and Olivia always gave good ideas to help people. I liked it when Olivia cut Chloe's dress to make a new one." Isabel, age 7

"Cuddle is very cute and mischievous. I think she's the most adorablest thing I've ever known and I wish she was my kitten. I really enjoyed this story." Ava, age 7

"My favourite bit was when the boy prepared to cut Olivia in half. I was really in suspense about what was going to happen! I like the way that Chloe learnt to become confident. I love that Cuddle is always able to solve problems." Carmen, age 6

"I wish I had a kitten like Cuddle because she is sooooo cute and can do a bit of magic. My favourite part of the story is when the girls appear in the show." Flora, age 7

Superstar Dreams

Cuddle

★ the cutest kitten ★

Superstar Dreams

by Hayley Daze
Illustrated by Ann Kronheimer
Cover illustrated by Amanda Gulliver

A catalogue record for this book is available from the British Library

Published by Ladybird Books Ltd
A Penguin Company
Penguin Books Ltd., 80 Strand, London WC2R 0RL, UK
Penguin Books Australia Ltd., Camberwell, Victoria, Australia
Penguin Group (NZ) 67 Apollo Drive, Rosedale,
North Shore 0632, New Zealand

001 – 10 9 8 7 6 5 4 3 2 1
Series created by Working Partners Limited, London WC1X 9HH
Text © Working Partners Ltd MMXI
Cover illustration © Working Partners Ltd MMXI
Interior illustrations © Ladybird Books Ltd MMXI

Special thanks to Elizabeth Galloway

ISBN: 978-1-40930-851-5
Printed in England

Mixed Sources
Product group from well-managed
forests and other controlled sources
www.fsc.org   Cert no. SA-COC-001592
© 1996 Forest Stewardship Council

To James and Victoria – good times

Cuddle the kitten has black-and-white fur,
A cute crooked tail, and a very loud purr.
Her two best friends, Olivia and Grace,
Know Cuddle's world is a special place!

Just give her a cuddle, then everything spins;
A twitch of her whiskers, and magic begins!
So if you see a sunbeam, and hear Cuddle's bell,
You can join in the adventures as well!

Contents

Chapter One
Treetop Tumble

A breeze rippled through the cherry tree, making its pink blossom dance. Grace's combat trousers and T-shirt were scattered with sweet-smelling petals.

"It's like being in a blossomy snowstorm," she called down to Olivia. "Climb up and see."

"I've never climbed a tree before,"

Olivia said, twirling one of her curls round and round a finger.

The girls were in Olivia's back garden. Grace was sitting in the cherry tree, while Olivia stood beside the trunk.

From her perch, Grace could see
her own back garden next door.
The roofs of the houses that lined
their street were still damp from a
recent rain shower. The sky over
Catterton was dark grey.

"Let's see if you can get up here
before it rains
again," Grace said.
"I'll help you."

"All right," Olivia
said. "Here goes."
Stretching up on to
the tips of her blue
sandals, she grabbed
the lowest branch.

"That's it," Grace said. "Now wrap your legs round the trunk and hold the next branch."

Olivia could see Grace's smiling  face through the leaves, framed by her shiny blonde hair. She stretched up for the branch, but her fingers slid over a patch of moss. With a shriek, she tumbled to the ground.

Grace scrambled down after her. "Are you okay?"

Olivia was lying face up, her black curls fanned out on the ground. "I'm fine," she said, smiling. "Now do you believe I can't climb trees?"

Grace pulled Olivia to her feet. "You just need to practise. Then you'll be able to climb like a cat!"

At that moment a sunbeam pushed its way through the clouds, scattering golden rays.

Olivia clapped her hands. "Oh! Do you think Cuddle's on her way?"

Cuddle was a cute kitten who had recently appeared in a beam of sunlight and taken the girls on a magical adventure.

Jingle jangle jingle.

"That's Cuddle's bell!" Grace cried.

The sunbeam shone on Olivia's bike, which was propped up against

the back of the house. A pink basket
was fixed to the handlebars. It
wiggled and jiggled, and Cuddle's
black-and-white face poked out. Her
green eyes sparkled in the sun.

"Hello, Cuddle!" both girls cried.

Olivia grinned. "The sunbeam
looks like a spotlight. Cuddle's a
movie star."

The kitten's bell jingled as she

sprang on to the bike's saddle. With a swish of her crooked tail, she leapt into Grace's arms and greeted her friends with a loud "Miaow!"

Grace hugged the kitten tightly. "You certainly live up to your name, don't you, Cuddle?" she said.

Purrrrrrrr, went Cuddle. She sounded like a tiny rumble of thunder.

The girls' skin tingled as if

Cuddle's whiskers were tickling them. Cuddle's purr grew louder and louder, and the girls started to giggle. They leaned into each other, the little kitten cradled between them.

Now they knew what would happen next – kitten magic! As Cuddle's purr rumbled on, the garden and the cherry tree faded away . . .

***

Grace's eyes fluttered open. She was lying on a hard surface in the pitch dark. She closed her eyes and tried opening them again, but it was no good. She couldn't see a thing.

"Olivia?" Grace asked. She could feel her heart thumping.

"I'm here," said Olivia. The two girls were lying side by side.

Olivia knew that Grace was afraid of the dark, and squeezed her friend's hand. *Where are we?* she wondered.

Grace reached inside the pocket of her combat trousers. Her fingers closed over her penlight and she flicked it on. A narrow beam of light shone out, and the girls could see that they were surrounded by walls.

Grace rapped the wall above them with her knuckles. It gave a hollow echo.

"That sounds like wood," she said. "I think we're inside some kind of box."

Olivia gulped. "We're trapped!"

Chapter Two
In the Spotlight

"Miaow!" said Cuddle, from somewhere by their feet. Grace shone the penlight at the kitten as she skipped up between them, her fur tickling their bare arms. She rubbed against Olivia's neck, then touched Grace's nose with her own.

"It's like she's telling us not to be scared," Grace said. She tried to stroke Cuddle's ears, but the kitten ducked out of the beam of light and Grace's fingers found the bend in her tail instead.

The girls jumped as a booming voice echoed over them. "Ladies and gentlemen! I'm glad you're all sitting down, as this next trick would have you falling over in amazement."

There was a distant ripple of laughter.

"Who's that?" Olivia whispered to Grace.

The voice continued. "May I present the Magic Box of Doom!"

"The Magic Box of Doom," Grace repeated. "Do you think that's where we are?" Her voice trembled.

Slam! A tiny door opened in the wall behind the girls' heads, letting in a stream of light. *Slam! Slam!*

Two more doors opened by their feet. *Slam! Slam!* A door opened on Olivia's side of the box, then another on Grace's.

The sudden brightness made the girls blink. Grace switched off her penlight and put it back in her pocket.

Cuddle walked up to the opening behind their heads and sniffed it.

"Good idea, Cuddle," Olivia said. "Let's find out where we are."

She wriggled head first towards the opening, arching her back like a caterpillar.

Grace shifted out of her way, using her elbows to move towards the bottom of the box.

"I can fit my legs through those two holes," Grace said. She stuck them through, waving her trainers around.

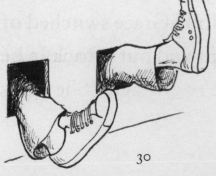

Olivia grabbed the rim of the tiny doorway. She pulled herself up so her head poked through the opening – and gave a gasp of amazement.

The box seemed to be mounted on a stand. It was painted blue, with a golden latch shaped like a lion's paw fixed just above the opening. Clusters of spotlights hung from the ceiling of a large room, behind a red velvet curtain that had been drawn up. To one side was a bank of seats, filled with rows of people. They were whispering to each other and pointing at her.

A grin spread over Olivia's face. "Grace, we're onstage!" She stuck her hand through one of the side openings and waved at the audience. "This is brilliant. I've always wanted to be an actress."

A boy a little older than Olivia and Grace was standing at the back of the stage. He was wearing a blue suit with a gold sash slung across his body. His black top hat was too big

for him and flopped down over
one ear. He was staring
at Olivia, his eyes wide
with surprise. She
realized he must be
the owner of the
booming voice.

The boy gave
himself a shake,
causing his top hat
to fall over the
other ear.

"Looks like
I've already got an
assistant," he said.

He drew out a long
shiny sword from his sash.

The audience gasped.

What's he going to do? thought Olivia.

"Ladies and gentlemen," the boy said, "I will now cut this girl in half!"

Chapter Three
Cuddle the
Conjuring Kitten

"Oh no!" Grace called from inside the box. "Please don't chop us in two!"

The boy's eyebrows shot up so high, they disappeared under the brim of his hat. To him it must have sounded like Olivia's tummy was talking.

He gripped the sword's handle tightly and raised it above his head.

Olivia noticed that he was red in the face as he spoke to the audience. "Now I've got my sword, we can get to the *point* of the trick."

The audience laughed. From somewhere offstage came a rattling drum roll.

Inside the box, Cuddle's ears twitched and Grace saw the kitten's green eyes flash. Cuddle pushed her furry body through one of the holes Grace's feet were sticking out of. Then she perched on the toe of one of her trainers.

The audience exclaimed in delight.

"Look at that kitten," Olivia heard an old lady say. "How cute!"

The boy shook his head as he tried to work out where Cuddle had come from. The top hat flopped down over both his ears.

"Ladies and gentlemen," he said, "a big hand – I mean a big paw! – for ..."

"Her name's Cuddle," Olivia whispered.

"A big paw for Cuddle the Conjuring Kitten!" he finished.

The audience clapped and cheered.

"Now," the boy said, "are you ready to be amazed by the Magic Box of Doom?"

"Yes!" the audience shouted.

Olivia held her breath. She felt Grace's hand wrap round one of her ankles. He wasn't really going to cut them in two, was he? *It's just a magic trick*, Olivia tried to convince herself.

The boy swung his sword towards the box. As it sliced through the air, Cuddle pounced on the lion's-paw latch. *Click!* The latch sprang open and the box fell apart, the walls and

lid crashing to the ground. Out
tumbled Olivia and Grace. Cuddle
jumped clear, landing beside them.

The boy dropped his sword in shock.

Olivia looked up at him. "We're sorry Cuddle ruined your magic trick," she said.

"She didn't ruin it," the boy replied. "She made it even better!"

He pulled Olivia and Grace to their feet, and turned to the audience. "It turns out I'm an even better magician than I realized. Instead of cutting a girl in half, I've doubled her!"

"I think that makes you a mathematician rather than a magician," Grace said with a grin.

The audience got to their feet, cheering and whistling. The boy

raised his arm above his head and
swept down in a bow, making his
top hat fall off. Grace bowed too,
and Olivia dropped into a deep
curtsy. Cuddle jumped inside the
top hat, just her little whiskered face
poking out.

Olivia nudged Grace. "I told you
Cuddle was a star!"

Chapter Four
Good Luck Charm

Grace squinted past the glare of
the spotlights. At the front of the
audience was a table with three
people sitting behind it. A large
silver star was fixed to the table,
with 'Star Maker' written across it in
swirly red letters.

"We're at a talent show," she said.
"They must be the judges."

Cuddle sprang off the stage, landing on the judges' table. Two of the judges, a woman in a purple dress and a man in a red jacket, stroked the little kitten. She rolled over in front of the third judge, a man with gelled hair and a tight white T-shirt, knocking over his nameplate. It said 'Larry'.

"Nice to meet you, Cuddle the Conjuring Kitten," Larry said, tickling her tummy. He looked up at the boy onstage.

"You've definitely got star potential," Larry said to the boy. "And so has Cuddle," he added, with a wink at the kitten.

As the curtain came down, the boy cried, "Thank you, Cuddle – you made my act *purr*-fect!"

Cuddle raced offstage with Grace and Olivia right behind her and darted through a half-open door.

"I wonder why she's taking us here," Olivia said, spotting a sign that said 'Dressing Rooms'.

Grace pushed open the door and stared in wide-eyed amazement. There were jugglers juggling, clowns laughing, gymnasts tumbling, dancers twirling, singers humming and at least two performing dogs.

Cuddle bounced up to a girl, who looked like she had stepped out of a history book, and leapt into her arms.

"Oh!" the girl exclaimed.

"Sorry. That's Cuddle and she's very friendly," Grace said.

The girl's face was as white as Cuddle's tummy. "Are you all right?" Olivia asked.

A woman was standing next to the girl, holding a book called *Poems by William Shakespeare*. She said, "Chloe's just nervous about performing her act. Aren't you, dear?"

Chloe nodded. She was trembling all over, from her red hair, which

was pinned up in a bun, to her long
emerald dress, right the way down
to her green shoes. Even her puffed
sleeves were shaking.

"I'll be all right as long as I have my
lucky charm," Chloe said. She held
out her hand to show the girls a chain
with a sparkling white jewel hanging
from it.

Cuddle batted it and watched it swing.
"It's beautiful," Olivia said.

"What's your talent?" Grace asked.

"Chloe's dressed as a girl from
Shakespeare's time," Chloe's mum said.
"She's reciting one of his poems for her
act."

A man burst through the door behind
them, holding a clipboard. He wore a
badge saying 'Stage Manager'.

"Is Hypno the Great here?" he asked. "It's his turn to perform."

Another man, dressed in long blue robes with an orange turban on his head, weaved his way through the sea of performers.

"There you are," the stage manager said. "You'll be Hypno the Late if you don't hurry."

Hypno whirled round. "I need to find my crystal first. I think a monkey took it. It's essential to my act." His eyes lit up as he saw the necklace sparkling in Chloe's hand. "That's perfect! Can I borrow it?"

Before Chloe could reply, Hypno grabbed the necklace from her and ran out to the stage.

"My lucky necklace!" Chloe cried. "I can't perform without it." Her eyes welled with tears.

"I'll get it back," Grace said. "Hypno, wait!"

She sprinted after him, her legs pounding as if she was aiming for the finishing line on Sports Day.

Without thinking, Grace ran across the stage towards him, but there was a creak of rope and a *whoosh!* of velvet. The stage curtain was going up!

Chapter Five
Cuddle Lends a Paw

Olivia, Cuddle, Chloe and her mum
watched from the wings of the stage
as Hypno gestured for Grace to sit
in a velvet chair. He sat down
opposite her.

Chloe's mum had her arms folded
crossly as she spoke to the stage
manager. "I want my daughter's
necklace back now!"

"Keep the noise down, please," he replied. "Hypno's about to begin."

"Don't worry," Olivia said quietly to Chloe. "We'll get your necklace back as soon as he's finished his act – whatever it is."

"Hypnosis," the stage manager whispered. "That's what his name's short for. He puts people into a very deep sleep."

"What if Grace isn't sleepy?" Olivia asked.

"It doesn't matter," the stage manager said. "He'll make her sleep and tell her to do funny things."

Olivia gulped. Would Grace be all right?

Onstage, Hypno held up Chloe's necklace between Grace's face and his own. He swung it gently.

"Keep your eyes fixed on the necklace," he intoned. "You'll soon be feeling tired."

Cuddle pushed between Olivia and Chloe and strolled on to the stage.

She stood behind Grace's chair,

blinking in the spotlights.

"Cuddle!" Olivia whispered.
"Come back!"

But the little kitten clambered
up the back of Grace's chair. Her
crooked tail twitched in time with the
necklace as it swung back and forth.

"You're getting sleepy," Hypno told
Grace. "Very sleepy. . ."

But his own voice began to sound

tired and his head swayed, following
the movement of the necklace.

Olivia watched Cuddle. The kitten
swished her tail back and forth, faster
and faster, and the necklace became a
gleaming blur. Olivia's eyes widened.
Cuddle was controlling it!

Hypno gave an enormous snore.
He tipped forward from his chair on
to the stage, where he curled up – fast
asleep.

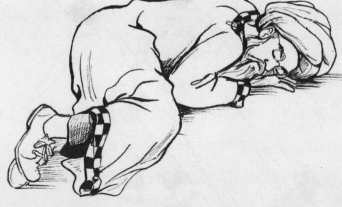

Olivia giggled. "Cuddle made Hypno hypnotize himself!"

The stage manager ran onstage, his face red. "Er, ladies and gentlemen! We seem to – um – have a problem."

The necklace was still in Hypno's hand. Before Grace could reach it, two men with Star Maker T-shirts hurried past her. They each took one of Hypno's arms and dragged him away.

"Stop!" yelled Chloe's mum, running after them. "That's my daughter's lucky necklace!"

Backstage, the stage manager rubbed his eyes. "Bring the curtain down, before anything else goes wrong!" As the curtain swished shut, Grace picked up Cuddle and joined Olivia and Chloe backstage.

"You need to get ready, Chloe," the stage manager called, glancing at his clipboard. "It's nearly your turn to go on."

Chloe shook her head so hard that her bun started to tumble down.

"Not without my necklace or my mum. I can't do it." Then she ran off.

Grace drew Olivia to one side.

"I know why Cuddle's brought us here," Grace whispered. "We've got to help Chloe perform – whether she has her lucky necklace or not."

Chapter Six
Chloe's Dream

Olivia, Grace and Cuddle raced after Chloe. She was fast and they couldn't keep up. They ended up in a central hallway with lots of small practice rooms leading off from it – but there was no sign of Chloe.

Grace whirled around. "Where could she have gone?"

Olivia looked inside one of the

rooms. A group of boys wearing
rollerskates and tracksuits was
practising, mixing skating moves with
breakdance spins and flips.

Chloe wasn't there. Grace ran into
the next room. A troupe of dancers in

multicoloured leotards and footless
tights was doing leaps and twirls.

"Have you seen a girl in a green
dress?" Grace asked. They shook
their heads.

Cuddle jumped out of Grace's
arms and trotted across the hallway.
One of the doors was open a crack.
She pushed her head through and

it swung open. Grace and Olivia followed her inside.

A girl with pink hair was holding an electric guitar. "One, two, three!" she cried and started playing, along with a girl on a keyboard and a boy on drums.

The Krazy Katz was painted on the largest drum. A crowd of other

performers was watching The Krazy
Katz practise. Cuddle gave a loud
miaow, and jumped into the lap of a
girl sitting cross-legged by the wall.
It was Chloe!

Grace and Olivia glanced at each
other. Chloe's eyes were red from
crying. They went to sit either side
of her, while Chloe ran her fingers
through Cuddle's whiskers.

"The judges will think this band is brilliant," Chloe said.

"They'll think you're brilliant, too," Olivia said. She remembered what Grace had told her about climbing trees. "Why don't you practise reciting the poem to us now? You might feel better."

Chloe sighed.

"The Shakespeare poem was my mum's idea. What I really want to do is sing."

"Then that's what you should do!" Grace said. "What's your favourite song?"

" 'Cat That Got the Cream', " Chloe replied.

"Sing it for us," Olivia said. "We'd really like you to."

Chloe's cheeks went pink, but she took a deep breath and began. It was a pop song the girls knew, and they tapped their feet in time. Cuddle swished her tail like a conductor's baton. Everyone turned to listen, and even The Krazy Kats stopped playing as Chloe launched into the chorus:

"Me and my friends, we're a team,
We flow together like fish in a stream.
We laugh and cry, play and dream,
And I feel like the cat that got the cream."

Everyone broke into applause.

"That girl can really sing," said the band's keyboard player.

Olivia clapped her hands and Grace put two fingers between her lips, giving a loud whistle. "Chloe, that was amazing!" Grace said. "You've got to sing for the judges."

"I can't," Chloe said sadly. Her eyes were filling with tears. "I haven't any music to sing along to. I can't wear this dress. I don't have my necklace. And–"

Olivia seized Chloe by the shoulders. "It'll be fine. You've got Grace, Cuddle and me to help."

Olivia looked Chloe's dress up

and down. "I know just how to make you the perfect costume. You'll look like a star! Won't she, Cuddle?"

Cuddle stared up at the three girls.

Then she bolted between their legs. Grace shook her head. "Where's that crazy kitten gone now?"

Chapter Seven
Cuddle Makes Some Noise

Grace followed Cuddle through the crowd that had gathered. The little kitten bounded towards The Krazy Katz and hopped on to the drummer's lap.

The

He was tall with a ripped T-shirt and a chain hanging round his neck. Grace thought he looked a little scary.

But the drummer's tough face melted into a smile. "Hello, kitty-cat," he said. "Do you want to play?"

Cuddle hopped on to one of the drums, making an echoing *boom*. She flicked her crooked tail in delight, and pounced on the next drum.

Boom! She sprang all over the drum kit, filling the room with noise. *Ba-boom, bang, boom, bang, boooooom!* She finished by swiping the cymbals with her front paw. *Craaaaaaash!*

The girl with pink hair laughed. "I guess she does want to play – play music!"

Grace picked up Cuddle. "I'm so sorry," she began.

But The Krazy Katz were clapping and cheering Cuddle's performance.

"Your kitten should be in our band," the girl with the keyboard said. "She sure is cute."

The pink-haired girl nodded. "Our lead singer has just quit," she said.

"We need a new member."

Grace could feel excitement bubbling inside her like lemonade. "Did you hear my friend Chloe singing?"

They all nodded. "She was brilliant," said the drummer.

"And do you know the song she sang?" Grace asked.

"'Cat That Got the Cream'?" the pink-haired girl asked. "It's my favourite." She strummed the opening notes on her guitar.

Grace beamed and hugged Cuddle. "You need a singer – and Chloe needs a band. Maybe she could sing with you?"

The three Krazy Katz grinned. "That would be fantastic!" the drummer said.

While Grace and Cuddle led the rock band through the busy practice room, Olivia put the finishing touches to Chloe's new outfit. She

had used the nail scissors she kept
in her sequinned bag to cut the
dress diagonally across, so it hung
longer on one side than the other, and
chopped off the sleeves. She brushed
out Chloe's red hair so it swept over
one of her shoulders.

Chloe twirled around
on the spot. "Thank you!
I feel like a rock star."

"Now all you need
is a band," Grace said
with a smile. "Chloe,
these are The Krazy
Katz."

"Hi, Chloe," the girl with pink hair
said. "We'd love you to sing with us."

"I'd like that!" Chloe replied.

Cuddle twitched her whiskers. Sparkly green cat brooches appeared on Chloe and the two Krazy Katz girls and a glittery green baseball cap appeared on the drummer's head. They matched Cuddle's shining eyes.

"Where did these come from?" Chloe exclaimed, stroking the

twinkling jewels in her brooch.

"Cuddle can do more than play the drums," Olivia said, scratching Cuddle behind her black-tipped ear. "She's a magic kitten!"

"Maybe Cuddle should be in the show," the girl with pink hair said. "She's definitely talented!"

The door to the practice room opened and the stage manager stuck his head round. "Chloe!" he called. "It's your turn to perform."

Grace squeezed Chloe's hand. "Come on, it's time to go."

But Chloe shook her head. "I can't do it," she said.

"There's nothing to worry

about," Olivia replied, putting an arm round her. "You've got a new outfit, a band – and an amazing voice."

"There's one thing I haven't got," Chloe said, looking at the floor. "My good luck charm."

"You don't need luck," Grace said. "You've got talent."

Chloe looked up. "Really?"

Olivia nodded. "And you've got me, Grace and Cuddle to cheer you on. Friends are the best lucky charm of all!"

Chapter Eight
A Starry Success

Olivia, Grace and Cuddle watched
as Chloe and The Krazy Katz
performed onstage. The crowd was
clapping along to the beat.

"Looks like my daughter doesn't
need this any more," a voice behind
them said. It was Chloe's mum,
smiling. She slid Chloe's lucky
necklace into her handbag.

Cuddle bounded across the stage and leapt on to the drummer's lap. "Look, Cuddle wants to be a rock star, too!" Grace said.

The pink-haired girl swung her guitar as she played, and Cuddle

tapped the cymbals with her paw.
Swish. Swish. Boom-boom-swish.

Then Chloe started to sing. Olivia and Grace peeked out from behind the curtains.

The judges were swaying along, and Larry was using his pen to tap out a rhythm on the table.

"She looks so happy," Chloe's mum said. "Thank you for helping her."

"That's okay," Grace replied. "It was fun."

The song ended with a long high note from Chloe, and a huge *craaaash* as Cuddle used both of her front paws to swipe the cymbals.

The audience leapt to its feet, cheering and applauding as Chloe confidently strode to the front of the stage and gave them a deep curtsy.

"Bravo!" yelled the comedian
magician, tossing his top hat into
the air.

Larry held up his hand and the
cheers faded away.

Grace linked her arm nervously through Olivia's. What would the judges say?

Larry's face was serious. He leant forward in his seat. "Chloe," he said, "do you know how that song made me feel?"

Chloe shook her head.

"Then I'll tell you," Larry began. The girls held their breath, but he suddenly grinned. "Like the cat that got the cream. I loved it!"

The audience erupted into applause. "Go, Chloe!" Olivia shouted as the girls whirled each other round.

Larry's white teeth gleamed.
"Congratulations, Chloe. You and
The Krazy Katz are stars!"

Chloe ran offstage where her mum
caught her in a hug.
"Well done," Grace said, patting
Chloe on the back. "You deserve it."

"It's all thanks to you," Chloe replied, "and Cuddle."

The little kitten pushed into the middle of the three girls. She bumped her furry head against Chloe's ankles, then weaved through Grace and Olivia's feet.

They could feel her purr shaking through them.

"It's time for us to go," Grace said. "Goodbye, Chloe!"

"Goodbye!" Olivia called.

Chloe and the Star Maker stage became a whirling blur of colour, and the girls shut their eyes.

***

When Grace opened her eyes again, she and Olivia were lying on the springy grass in Olivia's garden.

"That was so much fun," Grace said, giving a delighted wriggle. "Wasn't Chloe brave?"

"She was," Olivia agreed. "And now it's my turn to be brave. I'm going to climb the cherry tree!"

The two girls ran to the trunk. Grace swung on to the lowest branch then stretched out her hand.

Olivia grabbed it and Grace helped her scramble up.

"You're climbing the tree!" Grace cried.

Jingle jangle jingle.

Cuddle was sitting on the branch above them, surrounded by pompoms of blossom.

She held out a front paw as if she was waving goodbye, then disappeared in a haze of sparkles.

"Goodbye, Cuddle," the girls called. "See you soon!"

Olivia tucked a blossom behind her ear. "Do you know how sitting up here makes me feel?" she asked.

Grace laughed, and both girls shouted, "Like the cat that got the cream!"

Can't wait to find out
what Cuddle will do next?
Then read on! Here is the first chapter
from Cuddle's third adventure,
PRINCESS PARTY SLEEPOVER ...

Cuddle
★ the cutest kitten ★

Princess Party Sleepover

It was a warm summer's evening and Olivia's bedroom window was wide open. Purple wisteria flowers nodded against the sill and furry bumblebees buzzed around them, collecting the last of the day's pollen. The setting sun made the houses of Catterton glow a rosy pink.

"Our first sleepover!" Olivia

squealed, twirling in her pink ruffled nightie.

"I've never been to a sleepover before," Grace said, doing up the last button of her favourite star-patterned pyjamas. "What should we do first?" The girls flopped on to Olivia's bed, which had a fluffy pink duvet.

"Let's play princesses," Olivia suggested. She leapt to her feet, wobbling on her bed, and wrapped her duvet round her shoulders like a royal robe.

"Ta-dah!" she said and pretended to wave at her loyal subjects.

"Hello, your royal highness!" Grace said and bowed to Olivia.

"Now it's your turn," Olivia said, jumping down to sit beside Grace. "You'd make a lovely princess."

Grace shook her head, making her blonde ponytail fly about. "No way! Who wants to be a princess and have to wear dresses and go to boring parties? Yuck!"

Olivia stared open-mouthed at her friend. "I would love to be a princess, trying on all those lovely outfits and tiaras."

Suddenly, the setting sun sent a golden beam of light directly through the open window.

"Maybe Cuddle's coming!" Olivia said, looking down into her back garden. The girls couldn't wait to see the magical kitten again.

Cuddle always arrived in a sudden burst of sunshine and took them on amazing adventures.

A sound drifted through the window.

Jingle jangle jingle.

"That's her bell!" Grace cried.

The wisteria branch beneath Olivia's window was shaking, its flowers bobbing up and down. A tiny white tail with a kink in its black tip flicked out from the quivering leaves.

"Cuddle!" both girls shouted.

The kitten's green eyes flashed as she scrambled on to the window sill, the silver bell on her pink collar jangling. She sprang between the girls into Olivia's room, landing in the middle of the bed. "Miaow!"

Cuddle pawed Olivia's arm. Olivia scooped the kitten up, cradling her upside-down to show her tummy.

"Cuddle's purring," Olivia said, her eyes shining. "That means we're going on another adventure!"

"Where are you going to take us, Cuddle?" Grace asked, nuzzling Cuddle nose to nose.

Cuddle's purr grew louder and louder, buzzing like the bumblebees outside.

The girls' skin tingled all over,

making them giggle.

Grace and Olivia squeezed their eyes tightly shut.

"Here we go!" Olivia said.

***

To find out what happens next,
get your copy of
Princess Party Sleepover today!

Cuddle
the cutest kitten

Magical Friends

Meet Olivia, Grace and Cuddle
in their first adventure!

New friends Olivia
and Grace are
amazed when cute
kitten Cuddle
appears and whisks
them away to an
ancient Egyptian
pyramid. Can they
help Beset find the
Pharaoh's kitten
inside it?

Find out in MAGICAL FRIENDS...

Cuddle
the cutest kitten

Princess Party Sleepover

Who wants to be a princess?

Princess Victoria
doesn't. She'd much
rather be wearing old
clothes and climbing
trees. Can Cuddle,
Olivia and Grace
convince her that
being a princess
can be fun in time
for the royal ball?

Find out in PRINCESS PARTY
SLEEPOVER…

Cuddle
★ the cutest kitten ★

School of Spells

Join Cuddle, Grace and Olivia on
a magical school adventure!

Cuddle takes the
girls to a school
with a difference
– the pupils are
enchanted creatures
and the lessons are
magical! But will
they be able to help
a shy unicorn make
some friends?

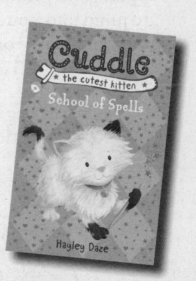

Find out in SCHOOL OF SPELLS...

Puddle
the naughtiest puppy

If you like Cuddle the Cutest Kitten you'll love Puddle the Naughtiest Puppy!

Puddle is a mischievous puppy who appears every time it rains. He only has to jump into a puddle to take cousins Ruby and Harry on a series of amazing magical adventures.

Why not begin your Puddle collection today?

Puddle
the naughtiest puppy

Magic Carpet Ride

Hayley Daze

Puddle
the naughtiest puppy

Toyshop Trouble

Hayley Daze

Puddle
the naughtiest puppy

Ballet Show Mischief

Hayley Daze

Puddle
the naughtiest puppy

Rainforest Hide and Seek

Hayley Daze

Puddle
the naughtiest puppy

Dragon Dance

Hayley Daze

Puddle
the naughtiest puppy

Magic Mayhem

Hayley Daze

Puddle
the naughtiest puppy

Pirate Surprise

Hayley Daze

Puddle
the naughtiest puppy

Animal Antics

Hayley Daze

Puddle
the naughtiest puppy

Christmas Snow Puppy

Hayley Daze

Puddle
the naughtiest puppy

Star of the School

Hayley Daze

Puddle
the naughtiest puppy

Holiday Musical

Hayley Daze

Caring for a cat

Grace, Olivia and Cuddle have lots of fun on their adventures together, but real cats and kittens need a lot of looking after. That's why our friends at Cats Protection are going to be joining us in each book to talk about everything a cat needs for a happy home life.

Caring for a cat is a big responsibility and one that the whole family can share. Cats Protection recommend that all cats have regular vet checks and vaccinations, and a diet of good quality tinned or dried cat food along with fresh water. Playing with your cat is also a great way for him to use up some of his energy, keep fit and healthy and keep his brain alert and active.

Always remember:
Cuddle is a magical kitten,
while real cats and kittens
are living animals who
need a lot of care,
love and attention.

What your cat needs at home

- A place for food and water
- Somewhere nice to sleep
- A scratching post
- Somewhere to hide
- Something they can climb on to sit and watch what is happening
- Some toys to play with
- A litter tray so they can go to the toilet

Congratulations – now you know all about what a cat needs to be happy in your home. Next time, we'll be learning all about a cat's behaviour. See you then!

Cats Protection is the UK's leading feline welfare charity. Cats Protection has been helping cats since 1927 and each year they help more than 215,000 cats and kittens, giving them the chance of a better life.
To find out more, please go to: www.cats.org.uk
For more cool cat facts, games and downloads, visit www.cats.org.uk/cats-for-kids

Spot the Cuddle Difference!

Here are two pictures of Cuddle and her friends.

Look at the first picture carefully, then look at the second.
Can you spot six tricky differences between them?

Hypno Pictures

Look carefully at the picture of Hypno the Great below. One of the pictures on the opposite page matches it exactly. Can you work out which one it is?

A

B

C

Answers at the end of the book

Cuddle
★ the cutest kitten ★

To find out more about the adorable Cuddle and her magical adventures, visit

www.ladybird.com/cuddlethekitten

Read hints and tips on how to look after your own cat from Cats Protection, plus download lots of fun activities.

Find more fantastic Ladybird titles at
www.ladybird.com

Answers to Cuddle Puzzles:
Spot the Cuddle Difference!: Cuddle's paws are no longer black; Grace has dots on her top; Grace has one black shoe; the sequins on Olivia's bag have disappeared; Olivia's left foot is missing and Olivia no longer has a star in her hair.
Hypno Pictures: B